Flood

Gillian McClure

Published in 2014 by Plaister Press
10 9 8 7 6 5 4 3 2 1
Copyright © Gillian McClure 2014
The moral right of the author/illustrator has been asserted

A CIP catalogue record for this book is available from the British Library

Design: Lisa Kirkham

Printed in Poland

Plaister Press Ltd
Registered address:
3 King Street, Castle Hedingham,
Halstead, Essex, CO9 3ER UK

www.plaisterpress.com

ISBN: 978-0-9565108-5-3

For Liv

pp
plaisterpress

It rained and it rained.
Water poured down from the sky.

Out in a field, Old Slodger the Ox
kept his head down, eyes to the ground,

and close by, Fussy Hen squawked and looked
this way and that for the Hungry Fox.

'I wish she'd shut up,'
thought Old Slodger
the Ox.

'Something's coming!' squawked Fussy Hen.
'It's the Hungry Fox. KICK HIM!'

'Oh, not again,' thought Old Slodger the Ox
and kept his head down,

eyes to the ground.

Not one of them saw the flood draw near ...

'He's going to eat me,' squawked Fussy Hen

and looked this way
and that

and then, stupidly,
into the eyes of
the Hungry Fox.

He held her in his

STARE

while Old Slodger the Ox
saw water swirl around his hooves.

The FLOOD was upon them with a *rush* and a **ROAR**.

The Hungry Fox was swept off his feet

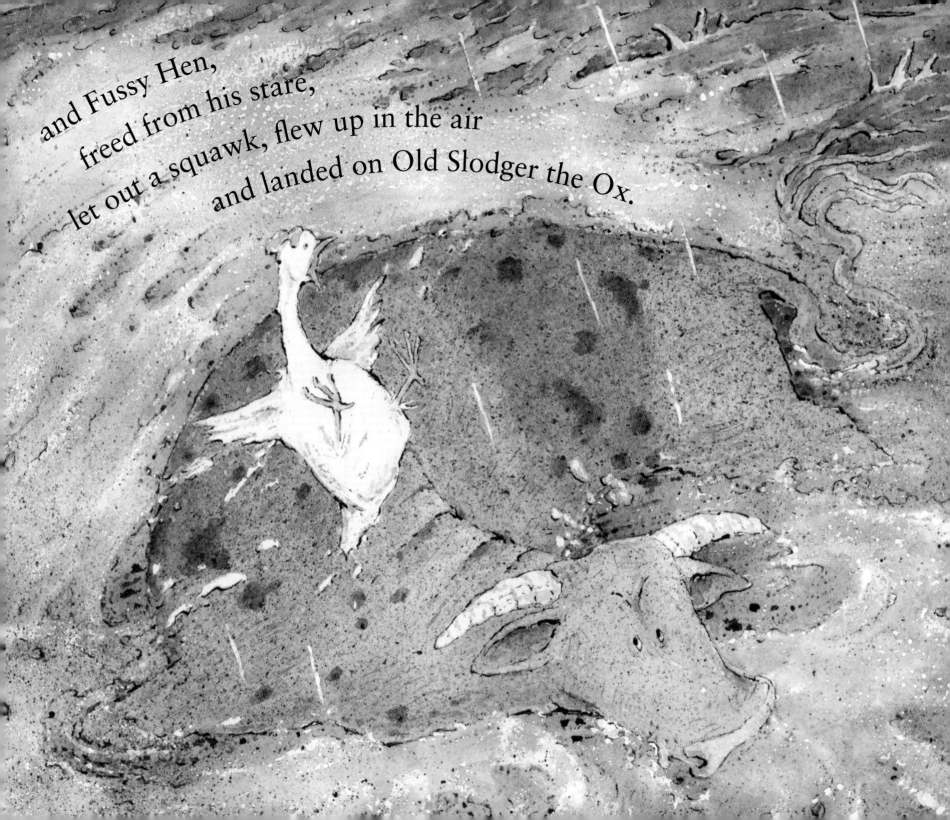

and Fussy Hen,
freed from his stare,
let out a squawk, flew up in the air
and landed on Old Slodger the Ox.

'Come back!' barked the Hungry Fox
and grabbed the tail of Old Slodger the Ox.

'Ow!' bellowed the ox and tried to shake off the fox but instead it was Fussy Hen who fell into the flood.

'Help!' she squawked, coming up for air.

Quickly, the Hungry Fox stuck out his brush and curling it round, caught Fussy Hen as she f l o a t e d by.

Now the fox had his hen
but he was still clinging on tight
to the tail of the ox,

who bellowed, 'Let go!'

and lifting his head, kicked out at the fox,

missed,

and found to his surprise he could swim.

But the flood was so big.
'Who will show me which way to go?'
wondered Old Slodger the Ox.

He heard a
squawk.

'Sounds like Fussy Hen,' he thought.

It *was* Fussy Hen,
caught on the end, in a red furry nest,

looking   this   way   and   that,

d o d g i n g
the eyes of the Hungry Fox.

'We're going in circles,'
she squawked.

'STRAIGHTEN UP!'

The Hungry Fox looked back,

tugged at the tail of Old Slodger the Ox

who bellowed,
'OW',
turned,

and Fussy Hen found to her surprise
she could steer.

'To the **left**.'

'To the right.'

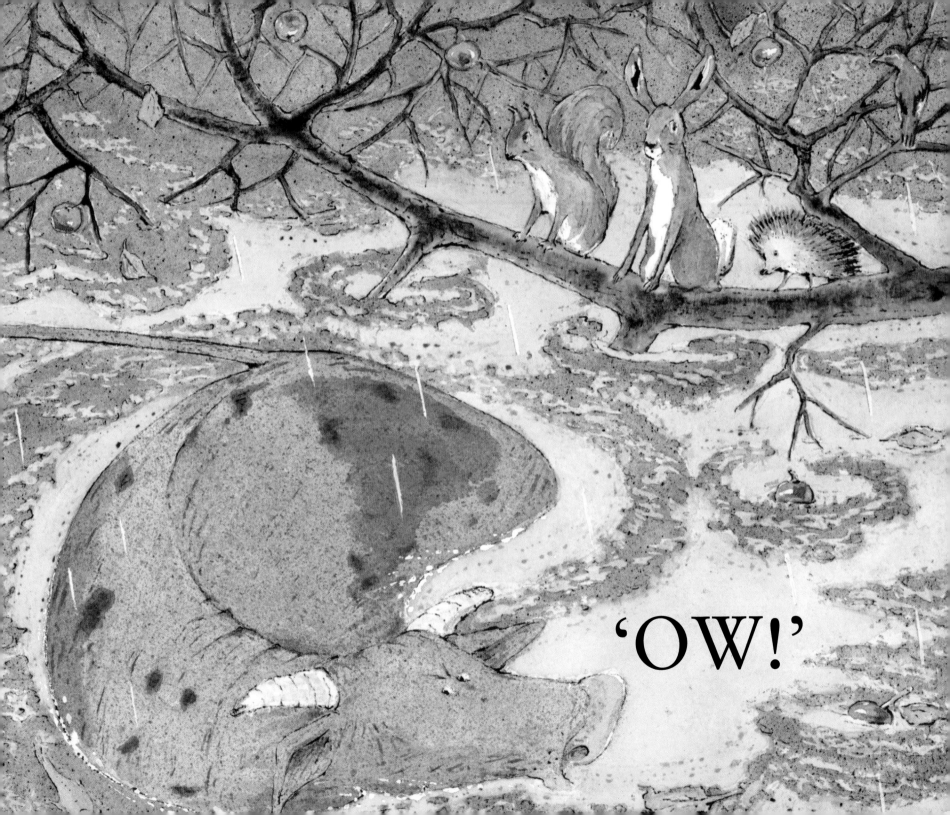

'OW!'

And so they went on, through the great flood,
steered by Fussy Hen, looking this way and that
from her nest at the back,

until they saw land.

Tired and cold, Old Slodger the Ox, the Hungry Fox
and Fussy Hen scrambled out of the flood

but there wasn't much
room on the land.

So they had to squash up close.

Then the rain stopped and Old Slodger the Ox thought, 'Maybe, after all, I won't kick the fox.'

And the Hungry Fox thought,
'Maybe, after all, I won't eat the hen.'

And Fussy Hen stopped squawking,
and stopped looking this way and that,
and was peaceful and quiet.

They sat together and watched as the sun came out
and slowly dried up all the rain
and the flood drew back and
there were fields again.